Fabulous Five-Minute Stories

# Off to the Moon!

Written by Stephanie Marbury

Illustrated by Tom Leigh

**Reader's Digest Young Families**

Billy's dad was putting Billy to bed. "I hope you had a good day, Son, and that you like your new pet," he said.

"Oh yeah, Dad. He's great. Thanks a lot, " said Billy, smiling weakly.

"Now, I know what you really wanted was a dog. But hey, gerbils make *great* pets! In fact, when I was your age, I had a gerbil."

Billy's dad got a misty look in his eyes. "His name was Squiggly. And Squiggly and I flew to the Moon."

Billy's eyes widened. "You did *what*?"

"I was on a field trip to the Space Center with my class," said Billy's dad. "A couple of astronauts-in-training were giving us a tour of the rocket ship that was scheduled to fly to the Moon. I had Squiggly in my pocket — you see, I took him everywhere. But just as my class was leaving the rocket pad, Squiggly squiggled out of my pocket and ran back into the ship. I just had to go after him.

"Of course, the two men who had been showing us around didn't know I was there," Billy's dad continued. "They were still aboard the rocket ship, having their coffee break. And then one of them accidentally set his coffee cup down on the LAUNCH button.

"'Uh, Tom?' one of them said to the other. 'Do you hear something?'

"'Yeah, Jeff,' Tom replied. 'If I didn't know better, I'd say it sounded like an engine firing up.'

"Jeff looked at Tom. Tom looked at Jeff. They rushed to one of the portholes. Well, we were on our way to the Moon.

"At first they didn't realize that Squiggly and I were aboard. They were too busy being upset about the fact that they were heading to the Moon.

"'I'm not ready to fly this rocket!' said Jeff. 'I'm only a few months into my astronaut training!'

"'Me, too,' agreed Tom.

"Suddenly I saw Squiggly. He was waggling his whiskers at me as he chewed something he was holding between his little paws. I stood up and tried to grab him, but the little fellow sidestepped away from me.

"'Hey! A kid!' yelled Jeff.

" 'Hi,' I said. 'I'm Jim.' I explained how I had been searching for Squiggly and that no, I certainly shouldn't have brought him along on the field trip, but that's how I accidentally found myself still on board. We all turned to look at Squiggly. He seemed to be settled in, chewing on a thick book, and much of it was already in little bitty pieces.

" 'Oh, no!' moaned Jeff. 'Your gerbil has chewed up the instruction manual! Now how are we ever going to get to the Moon and back?'

"By then we had left Earth's atmosphere. And because Earth's gravity wasn't pulling on us anymore, we all floated around the ship. I thought it was fun, but Jeff and Tom still seemed pretty worried about everything.

"The ship lurched and swayed a few times and seemed in danger of stalling out. The three of us hung on for dear life. But then suddenly everything smoothed out. The engine purred like a sports car's.

"'Hey! Look at the gerbil!' said Jeff. 'It's working the controls!'

"We looked. Squiggly was flying the rocket!

"I guess Squiggly must have read the instruction manual thoroughly before he chewed it up, because he was definitely in charge.

"With Squiggly flying the rocket, we landed safely on the Moon. The four of us put on moon suits, got out of the rocket ship, and actually bounced around on the surface. We were the first humans and gerbil to set foot and paws on the Moon. And Squiggly was having a fine time squiggling around the lunar rocks.

"Eventually, we got back on board, and Squiggly took over the controls again. He flew us safely back to Earth, with Jeff and Tom pitching in whenever they could.

"After we'd landed safe and sound, Tom and Jeff came and shook my hand. Then they patted Squiggly's tiny head.

"'Thanks, you two,' Jeff said. 'I don't know how we could have flown this rocket without your help. But, uh, we're going to say that this was just a little training mission, not an official trip to the Moon. Is that okay with you?'

"'That's fine, sir,' I replied. 'Squiggly and I were happy to be able to help out.'

"So that's why our trip didn't get on television or into the newspapers. But that never mattered to me. I have always been proud of what Squiggly did.

"So you see, Billy," said Billy's dad, "gerbils really do make great pets. And they are much smarter than anyone ever thinks."

Billy stared at his father, his eyes round with astonishment. His father kissed him good night, and then he left the room.

Billy turned toward his gerbil with new interest. He got
out of bed and padded over to the cage.

Then he took a book from the shelf and slipped it into the cage. "Good night, Squiggly Junior," Billy whispered.